When I grow up

Story by Beth Johnson

Illustrations by Mark Weber

Dr. Judith Nadell, Series Editor

It is Career Day in Mrs. Hall's class.

Many grown-ups have come to talk about their jobs.

The children can't wait to hear about the different careers.

A photographer talks about his career.

He takes pictures of different people and places.

Kendra thinks his job sounds great.

"When I grow up, maybe I'll be a photographer," she thinks.

A police officer talks about her career.

She helps people stay safe.

Derek thinks her job sounds great.

"I might be a police officer some day!"

he thinks.

A doctor talks about her career.

She helps sick people feel better.

Victor thinks her job sounds great.

"I bet I would be a good doctor," he thinks.

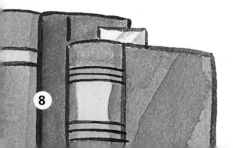

A flower shop owner talks about his career.

He makes people happy with flowers.

Jasmin thinks his job sounds great.

"I would like to own a flower shop, too!"

she thinks.

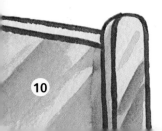

The children ask many questions.

They want to know everything about

the different careers.

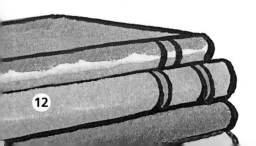

That night, the children have